Sallie Gal

and the Wall-a-Kee Man

Shelia P. Moses

illustrated by Niki Daly

Scholastic Press
New York

Text copyright © 2007 by Shelia P. Moses.
Illustrations copyright © 2007 by
Niki Daly. All rights reserved. Published
by Scholastic Press, an imprint of
Scholastic Inc., *Publishers since 1920.*
SCHOLASTIC, SCHOLASTIC PRESS, and associated
logos are trademarks and/or registered
trademarks of Scholastic Inc. • No part
of this publication may be reproduced,
stored in a retrieval system, or transmitted
in any form or by any means, electronic,
mechanical, photocopying, recording, or
otherwise, without written permission of
the publisher. For information regarding
permission, write to Scholastic Inc.,
Attention: Permissions Department,
557 Broadway, New York, NY 10012.
LIBRARY OF CONGRESS
CATALOGING-IN-PUBLICATION DATA
Moses, Shelia P. Sallie Gal and the
Wall-a-kee Man/by Shelia Moses;
illustrated by Niki Daly. —1st ed. p. cm.
Summary: More than anything, Sallie
Gal wants pretty ribbons to wear in
her hair, but she knows that they
cannot afford them and Momma has
too much dignity to accept charity.
ISBN-13:978-0-439-90890-0
ISBN-10: 0-439-90890-6
[1. Conduct of life—Fiction. 2. African
Americans—Fiction. 3. North Carolina—
History—20th century—Fiction.] I. Daly,
Niki, ill. II. Title. PZ7.M8475Sal 2007
[Fic]—dc22 2006033171 • 10 9 8 7 6 5
4 3 2 1 07 08 09 10 11 • Printed in
U.S.A. 23 • First edition, September
2007 • The display type was set in
Latino Samba and Latino Rumba. The text
type was set in 13.5-pt. Garamond.
Illustrations were done in digital media.
Book design by Marijka Kostiw

This book is dedicated

to Ronnetta Moses

and to all the

little boys and girls

who knew

the Wall-a-kee Man

–S.M.

To David Small —

a friend

and fellow sketcher

–N.D.

Table of Contents

1 . . . The Storm

Sallie Gal woke up with a great big smile on her face.

The wind had blown hard on Cumbo Road last night. So hard that the tops of the pine trees bent all the way to the ground. So hard that the wind blew Momma's old washtub off the back porch and over to the clothesline. So hard that the cotton stalks came out of the ground and blew all the way to the end of Cumbo Road. The cotton bows had blown all over the yard and the fields. That was the best part of all. Now Sallie Gal wouldn't have to chop cotton today!

Sallie Gal was happy. She knew her cousin Wild Cat would be happy, too. Both girls hated chopping. Especially when they had to work Saturday 'til noon. They wanted to spend their Saturdays playing instead. Besides, chopping the hard ground to get the weeds out of the fields made their hands hurt.

Sallie Gal would soon be nine years old, like Wild Cat. The girls spent part of their summer vacation working in the cotton fields. That is what all the kids on Cumbo Road did when school was out.

From Monday to Friday, they got to the fields at six o'clock in the morning. And they worked all day until six o'clock at night. On Saturdays they worked until noon. No wonder Sallie Gal and Wild Cat were so happy that most of the weeds and the cotton had blown away. Now they had all morning long to play double Dutch!

Sallie Gal jumped into her clothes and raced out the door to find Wild Cat. Sallie Gal and Wild Cat were always ready to play after a storm!

2 · · · Double Dutch

"**H**ey, Wild Cat," Sallie Gal called out as she jumped off the wooden porch.

Wild Cat poked her head out of her bedroom window. She had a big smile on her face, too. She had the same idea as Sallie Gal.

"Hey, Sallie Gal," Wild Cat answered. She ran

out her front door and cut across the grass that grew between their houses.

Wild Cat was not only Sallie Gal's favorite cousin — she was also her very best friend. Wild Cat's real name was Alice. But everybody on Cumbo Road called her Wild Cat because she had big, bright green eyes like a cat. They had lived right next door to each other since the day they were born, and they did everything together.

Wild Cat was one month and five days older than Sallie Gal, so she thought that she held all rights to being the boss. Especially when they did double Dutch.

Without saying another word, the girls ran around Sallie Gal's house to the other side where the jump rope hung between two trees. It wasn't really a jump rope. It was Momma's clothesline. But Momma was in the house cleaning up. And because they didn't have a real jump rope, Momma's clothesline rope would just have to do.

"Hold that log, girl," Wild Cat said, glancing around at the house to make sure the coast was clear. Momma didn't like sharing her clothesline. She said the girls were always getting it tangled up and dirty. So they had to be especially careful not to mess it up.

Wild Cat made Sallie Gal hold the wood log still. Otherwise it would rock back and forth when she stood on it. Momma was keeping that log to burn for heat this coming winter. She

always saved things for a rainy day. With Sallie Gal's papa away in the War, and with having to send money to Grandma Bee — who was Papa's momma — Momma said there would be lots of rainy days this winter.

Wild Cat was standing on the log because she wasn't tall enough to reach the clothesline. Sallie Gal wasn't even tall enough to reach it while standing on the log. So it was always Wild Cat's job to do the tying and the untying. Wild Cat untied the clothesline from the tree. Together the girls doubled the rope. They tied one end back around the tree because they did not have anyone to hold the other end.

"You go first," Sallie Gal said while holding her end of the rope.

Going first was music to Wild Cat's ears.

She smiled a big smile as Sallie Gal turned the rope.

"One, two, buckle my shoe," the girls sang as Wild Cat jumped.

Sallie Gal was a better double Dutch jumper. But Wild Cat was a show-off. If Wild Cat was not showing off her jump rope skills or her fancy dresses, she was showing off her hair ribbons. Every day she got to wear pretty hair ribbons she tied at the end of each ponytail that fell on her shoulders. Wild Cat's Aunt Lillie Mae was a school-teacher in Paterson, New Jersey. She sent Wild Cat a box with pretty dresses and matching hair ribbons four times a year. A box arrived at the beginning of every season. Wild Cat always had some new show-offy thing from the other side of her family. But it was those show-offy ribbons that drove Sallie Gal crazy.

As Sallie Gal turned the rope, Wild Cat jumped higher and higher. Wild Cat's long ponytails flew up toward the sky. On the end of each ponytail she had tied hair ribbons in every color of the rainbow.

More than anything, Sallie Gal wished she had hair ribbons just like Wild Cat's. She wanted them even more as she watched them bounce up and down in the bright sunlight.

If only Sallie Gal could ask her momma to buy her some. But she knew Momma would never waste money on silly things they didn't really need. Like hair ribbons. She could hear Momma now. There were too many things that they did need. Like fixing things around the house. And like fixing the car.

The car stopped working right after Papa left

for the War in Vietnam. So Momma's brother, Uncle Willie, shared his black Ford with her. Well, he used to, anyway. Now *that* car was broken down, too. Grass had started to grow around the wheels and birds built a nest under the front left tire. Momma said Uncle Willie was driving too fast and blew the motor. Uncle Willie said Momma was driving their car with no oil and she burned up the engine.

Whoever did whatever, Momma said they'd get it fixed as soon as they picked enough cotton this fall to pay the bill. So Sallie Gal didn't dare ask for those hair ribbons. Not now, anyway.

Wild Cat was really jumping high today as Sallie Gal turned the rope. Faster and faster Sallie Gal turned. She watched as Wild Cat jumped. Those pretty ribbons looked like the rainbow after a big rain.

"My turn, Wild Cat," Sallie Gal said.

Wild Cat ignored her and kept on jumping.

"One, two, buckle my shoe," Wild Cat began again. She said that she was the oldest, so she could jump the longest. She jumped around and tossed her head from side to side as she sang. Her hair ribbons swung back and forth. Wild Cat knew how good those new hair ribbons looked, too.

"Three, four, out the door!" Wild Cat continued.

Sallie Gal wanted to stop turning her end of the rope, but her momma said she had to always be nice to her company. So she kept on turning.

"Come on, Wild Cat," Sallie Gal said again. But Wild Cat just kept on jumping.

"Five, six, pick up sticks," sang Wild Cat.

"Stop jumping, Wild Cat!" Sallie Gal finally said. "It's my turn!"

Just as Wild Cat began to sing, *"Seven, eight, lay them straight,"* Sallie Gal stopped turning the rope altogether, and Wild Cat looked at her with surprise in her green eyes.

"That's not nice, Sallie Gal, I am your company."

Wild Cat did not want to, but she took the rope and turned it for Sallie Gal.

"Faster!" Sallie Gal called into the morning air. Sallie Gal might not have fancy hair ribbons on

her braids, but she could certainly show Wild Cat who could jump double Dutch better than anyone on Cumbo Road.

Miss Brown, Miss Brown went to town. . . .
Ate some candy and came back 'round!

Faster and faster. Up and down, and up and down. Sallie Gal's feet crisscrossed as fast as lightning. She jumped like she had rubber legs. As she jumped, she imagined those rainbow ribbons

bouncing and swinging from the ends of her braids. Higher and higher she jumped — until she saw a car she'd never seen before coming down the dusty dirt road.

Maybe it's Papa, Sallie Gal thought to herself.

Then she saw it was a station wagon. A big white station wagon. It was pulling up the driveway and coming to a slow stop. THE WALLACE

COMPANY was written on the side of the car in big letters.

"Who is that?" Wild Cat asked.

"I don't know," said Sallie Gal, trying to catch her breath. "I never saw that car before."

Wild Cat dropped the jump rope. Together the girls ran to the front yard to meet the stranger.

3 • • •The Wall-a-kee Man

When the dust settled, the stranger rolled down his window. He was a white man with gray hair, gray eyes, and little black glasses. He had on a navy blue suit like the menfolks on Cumbo Road wore to church on Sunday.

"Good morning, ladies," he said as he peeked over the top of his glasses.

"Mornin'," Sallie Gal and Wild Cat said together.

"By any chance is your momma at home?"

Before they could answer the stranger, Momma was out on the front porch giving Sallie Gal and Wild Cat that "go in the house" sign with her eyes.

The Wallace Company

Sallie Gal and Wild Cat didn't want to miss any excitement. Strangers *never* came to Cumbo Road. So Sallie Gal and Wild Cat ran around the house like they were going in the back door, but they didn't. Instead, they went back around the other side of the house to listen from behind the bushes.

"Are you Miss Ida Mae?" the man asked.

"Yes, I am," Momma answered in her most polite voice. "How can I help you?"

"Sorry to bother you, Miss Ida Mae. I'm James Wallace and I own The Wallace Company. I told Mr. Mason from the grocery store in town that I was looking for some new customers who had trouble getting to town on Saturdays. He told me to come and see you. Said your car was broken down. He was concerned about you getting your groceries. He thinks a lot of you, Miss Ida Mae."

"Well, that's real nice of him, sir," Momma said. "Mr. Mason been really nice since my husband has been away at the War. But I get to his store when I can and I get my groceries 'on time.' Don't have any money to do otherwise," Momma said.

Most of the colored folks on Cumbo Road got their groceries on credit — which they called "on time." They got what they needed from the store. Then they paid it back over a period of time.

"That will be just fine," Mr. Wallace said. "Because Mr. Mason went down his list of customers and told me that you are one of the finest people he knows. He said you pay him real good. Paying on time is fine with me."

Momma had so much pride that she dared not

pay a living soul on this earth past when she promised to pay.

Momma peeked through the window of the man's station wagon. Sallie Gal and Wild Cat were stretching their necks like peacocks trying to see, too. It was packed full with food, clothing, and bedspreads in every color. Pink bedspreads, blue bedspreads — and even polka-dot ones. Momma had never seen a polka-dot bedspread before. Anything you could think of, he had it in his car! Even though she said she didn't want to buy anything, Momma was looking hard at all those goods.

Sallie Gal wished she could walk up to that car window to see if he had some ribbons.

"Why don't you just pick a thing or two, and see how this works out," Mr. Wallace said.

Momma eyed a pair of white kitchen curtains with roses on them that she needed real bad. Mr.

Mason from the grocery store did not sell curtains.
And Momma knew it would be a long time before
she could get to Sears up in Rocky Mount again.
Momma paid fifty cents to whoever drove her to

town. So even though she hated getting things on time from a new person, she picked out a few items anyway.

Sallie Gal and Wild Cat watched as Momma

got a bag of sugar, two cans of milk, and curtains for the kitchen window. Everything together cost $3.67. That was a lot of money. Almost what Momma made working one whole day in the fields. Sallie Gal made a little bit of money working in the fields. But she wasn't allowed to spend it. She had to give it all to Momma for her school clothes and for things they needed in the house. Momma would give Sallie Gal the change, if there was any. But there never was.

The man made some notes in his black notebook and gave Momma a receipt.

"May I pay you fifty cents a week?" Momma asked.

"That will work fine, Miss Ida Mae," the man answered. "I have known Mr. Mason for twenty years. If he says you are good on your word, then that's enough for me. I will see you next week."

As soon as the man pulled off, the girls ran over to Momma to see what she'd bought from the stranger.

"Who was that, Momma?" Sallie Gal asked, like she didn't hear anything that just happened.

Wild Cat looked at the writing on the back of the car that said THE WALLACE COMPANY. "He's the Wall-a-kee Man," she read slowly.

Sallie Gal and Momma just smiled at each other because they knew that Wild Cat was always messing up names. They liked the sound of Wall-a-kee Man, though. So the name stuck.

"Well," said Momma, "the Wall-a-kee Man is kind of a traveling store. We can pick out a few things each week when he comes. And I can pay him on time. Like we do at Mr. Mason's store. But we'll save money since we won't have to pay to get there."

Sallie Gal smiled wide as she and Wild Cat followed Momma around the side of the house to the kitchen door. Sallie Gal thought about Wild Cat's ribbons. "Does the Wall-a-kee Man sell hair ribbons?" she asked.

"I don't know what . . ." Momma began. But before she could say another word, a big frown came over her face. On the ground next to a big mud puddle lay Momma's good clothesline!

"SALLIE GAL!" Momma shouted. She picked up her clothesline and inspected it. Luckily, no mud had gotten on it. "You and Wild Cat hang my clothesline back up right now!"

"Yes, ma'am," they whispered together. Without another word about hair ribbons, Sallie Gal held the log still while Wild Cat climbed on to hang

the clothesline back between the trees.

And that was the way it stayed — until the next time they wanted to do double Dutch.

4 • • • Picking Cotton

When Monday morning came, Sallie Gal and Wild Cat went back to work in the fields. Momma and Wild Cat's momma, Aunt Annie, were farther down the field with the other grown-ups. They could chop much faster than the children.

Wild Cat's Aunt Lillie Mae's boy, Rabbit, was there, too. He was visiting for the summer all the way from Paterson, New Jersey. He was hard at work in the fields with the girls.

"It's burning hot out here," Sallie Gal complained, wiping the sweat from her face.

"Tssssssssss," said Wild Cat, touching her finger to the hot metal blade on her chopping hoe. "You can fry pancakes on this hoe."

Rabbit didn't complain at all. He just kept on working. Rabbit was a city boy with country ways. The other city cousins who came for the summer always sat in the house until it was time to go back North. They hated the country sun and working in the burning hot fields.

But not Rabbit. Every summer when he came, he worked just like all the other country folks. He ran and jumped and played so much, folks forgot his name was Bennett and they nicknamed him Rabbit.

That morning, the sun beat down on their straw hats. The ground was very hard. Sallie Gal's hands were already hurting. The ground was so hard that every time she hit into it with the chopping hoe, the wood handle rubbed harder on her fingers.

The storm on Friday night had blown most of the cotton stalks and the cotton bows away. But the rain had made the weeds grow wild. So there was even more work to be done clearing them away. Mr. Coolie, the man who owned the land, said that all the weeds needed to be cleared out of the fields before cotton picking time in late September. There was not much cotton left, but what there was had to be picked and sold by Christmas.

As she worked, Sallie Gal got her mind on her hair ribbons and the Wall-a-kee Man again.

"Wild Cat," Sallie Gal began. "What do you think Momma would say if I asked her if I could

spend some of my work money on hair ribbons from the Wall-a-kee Man?"

Wild Cat stopped chopping and looked at Sallie Gal. "Sallie Gal, you know how your momma is. Your field money is for your school clothes. As soon as you ask she is going to say no."

"I'll never know if I don't ask," Sallie Gal said. She dropped her chopping stick and ran down the field to catch up with Momma.

Momma was talking to Aunt Annie.

"Momma, Momma!" Sallie Gal called.

"Child, don't you hear me talking to your Aunt Annie?"

Sallie Gal looked down at her old sneakers. "I'm sorry, Aunt Annie. Excuse me."

"It's all right, Sallie Gal," Aunt Annie said. "You go ahead, talk to your momma."

"What do you want, child?" Momma said. "You are supposed to be working."

"Momma, can I get some hair ribbons from the Wall-a-kee Man? Maybe I can use a little bit of my field money?"

Momma never stopped chopping around the cotton stalks. She always tried to get every weed out. She said it keeps the snakes out of the fields and it makes it easier to pick the cotton in the fall.

"Now, Sallie Gal, you know that we don't have money for extra things you don't need. Your papa is away at war. And your grandma needs some of the money for doctor bills and food. We have to save for bad times. Rainy days will surely come. We need food and wood and clothes. No extra things 'til your papa comes home."

Sallie Gal could tell she was making her momma

sad talking about Papa. She didn't want her to be
sad. She just wanted her ribbons.

"I was just wondering, Momma."

"Wondering doesn't do you any good, child.

You have to help yourself if you are going to get anything in this world. So keep chopping and maybe, just maybe, we will have some money left after we buy your school clothes and shoes."

"Yes, ma'am," Sallie Gal said. She knew there wouldn't be any money left after they bought school clothes and shoes. She would be lucky if she even made enough for school things. She walked away with her head down.

"What did your momma say?" Wild Cat asked as soon as Sallie Gal got back to her slowpoke cousins.

"She said I need to help myself," Sallie Gal said sadly.

"Maybe you could make some extra money for yourself," said Rabbit.

"How am I going to do that?" Sallie Gal asked.

"Up in Paterson the kids sell lemonade when

they want to make extra money. If you can get some sugar and lemons, you can make lemonade and sell it to people passing by."

"Boy," Wild Cat said, "you are not in Paterson, New Jersey. You are on Cumbo Road. Do you see any cars passing us?"

"A few," Rabbit answered with a laugh.

But Sallie Gal liked the idea. Soon Wild Cat did, too. And when it was time to eat lunch, Sallie Gal and Wild Cat were both excited about making plans.

"Rabbit, can you make me a lemonade stand?" Sallie Gal asked as they ate their cold beans from the can.

"I can't help you, because I am going to work in the tobacco field with the men tomorrow," Rabbit said. "But there's an old crate in the barn. You can use that."

"We can put our stand at the end of the road every day," Sallie Gal said. "Then, when the men come back from the tobacco field over in Rocky Mount, they can stop."

"That's a great idea," said Wild Cat like it was her own idea. "They are always hot and thirsty after a day's work."

"And Momma's got plenty of lemons," Sallie Gal added. "She trades her eggs for Miss Sadie's lemons." Miss Sadie lived down the road.

"Lemons?" Rabbit said. "Where did Miss Sadie get lemons from?" Rabbit asked like they only had lemons in Paterson.

"Her sister lives all the way in Florida," Sallie Gal answered. "She sends her lemons off the tree in her backyard."

The girls decided they would ask Momma for some sugar that she got from the Wall-a-kee Man and pay her back later. And they could use Aunt Annie's old pickle jars for glasses.

As the children finished their lunch, their eyes danced with excitement. Sallie Gal loved their new plan.

"Our lemonade stand is going to work, Wild Cat," Sallie Gal said as she walked back to the field.

5 . . . Making Lemonade

The next day, all Sallie Gal and Wild Cat talked about was their new lemonade business. They talked and talked as they walked up and down the cotton rows trying to get the weeds out. Rabbit was working with the men in the tobacco field today, so he wasn't there to get in their business. The time went very slowly. It felt like the day would never end.

When six o'clock finally came, the girls ran home from the field. They dragged the old wood crate from the barn all the way to the end of Cumbo Road. Then they raced back to Sallie Gal's house.

Momma smiled when she heard their plan. She loaned Sallie Gal an old pillowcase to cover the crate. And she helped them make lemonade in her old glass milk jug. Sallie Gal thought the jug was ugly so she went into the kitchen cupboard. She saw Momma's good glass pitcher.

"Can we borrow this?" Sallie Gal asked.

Momma did not look happy. "That is my good pitcher."

"We'll be careful," Sallie Gal promised.

Momma looked at her pitcher. Then she looked at Sallie Gal.

"Okay," she said. "Take it. But if you break it, you'll have to pay for it." She poured the lemonade out of the milk jug and into the sparkling glass pitcher. The lemonade looked cold and tasty.

"Thank you, Momma," Sallie Gal said. She grabbed the pitcher and rushed toward the door.

"You better hold that with both hands," Momma warned. "And don't run!"

"Okay," Sallie Gal promised. "Don't worry. I won't break it."

"You best not," Momma said. "You already owe me fifty cents for the sugar. And that pitcher cost two dollars from Sears. Your papa gave it to me. It's the finest thing in this kitchen."

"I'll be careful, Momma," Sallie Gal said as she held the pitcher tight with both hands and walked slowly up to the end of Cumbo Road to meet Wild Cat.

Wild Cat had already set up the lemonade stand. She lined up the pickle jars in a neat row. She even put up a sign that said:

The girls sat down to wait. No one came. Sallie Gal and Wild Cat were hot and tired. They waited some more. Still no one came.

"Sallie Gal, I think we should drink a little of the lemonade because it is hot out here," Wild Cat said.

"Yes, I think we should," Sallie Gal agreed as she poured them each a half glass. The cold ice and the sweet lemonade tasted so good. When no one came by, Sallie Gal poured them each another half glass.

Two cars passed, but they did not stop. Momma and Aunt Annie were going to be calling them to come in soon for supper, and they had not made one dime.

Finally a car drove down Cumbo Road. It came to a stop in front of them.

"Papa!" Wild Cat said with a big smile.

Uncle Willie got out of Mr. Sammy's car. Uncle Willie walked with a limp that he had had since he was a child. The limp kept him from having to go to the War in Vietnam with Papa.

"Get out of the car, Sammy, and buy some lemonade from these two lovely ladies," Uncle Willie said.

Mr. Sammy got out of the car and smiled at the girls.

Although most of the ice that Momma had put in the pitcher had melted, the thirsty men gulped down the lemonade in one big drink.

"Want a glass of lemonade?" Uncle Willie asked Rabbit.

Rabbit was looking out of the window at the pretty pitcher.

"It's on me." Uncle Willie winked.

"Thank you, sir," Rabbit said. But Rabbit was barely able to move after a hard day of work in the tobacco field with the men.

Wild Cat poured Rabbit a full glass of lemonade.

"Take it to him, Wild Cat," Uncle Willie said.

Even though she did not want to, Wild Cat walked over to the car and gave Rabbit his glass of lemonade.

Wild Cat could not help sticking her tongue out at Rabbit.

"Well, we best be getting home to have supper. And you ladies should, too," said Uncle Willie as he got back into his car.

As the men drove down the road, the girls packed up for the day.

"Wild Cat," Sallie Gal said. "We only made fifteen cents. We didn't even make enough to pay Momma for the sugar."

Wild Cat looked down at the money jar. "Why don't you just wear *my* hair ribbons?" she suggested. "Then we won't have to do all of this work."

"Thank you, cousin," Sallie Gal said. "But you know how Momma is about taking charity from other people. Anyway, it's only the first day. We will make more tomorrow."

All week, the girls set up their lemonade stand and waited for the field workers to come by. Every day they had the same customers. And every day they made the same fifteen cents. But whenever Sallie Gal thought about the hair ribbons she was going to buy, she forgot all about how hard she was working.

6 • • • Broken Pieces

On Saturday morning the sun beat down hot on the fields. Once again, the children were hard at work. They only had to work until noon today. And when noontime came around, they couldn't get home fast enough.

Sallie Gal took a bath in the big silver washtub in her room. The Wall-a-kee Man would be paying Momma a visit at one o'clock. And Sallie Gal couldn't wait to ask him about the ribbons.

After her bath, Sallie Gal put on clean blue jeans and a white shirt. Wild Cat and Rabbit bathed and changed, too. When they were all clean and dressed in their Saturday clothes, they sat on Sallie Gal's front porch and waited for the Wall-a-kee Man.

Usually, Rabbit worked in the fields with the menfolks on Saturday. But not today. Rabbit wanted to see the Wall-a-kee Man for himself. He had never seen a traveling salesman before in Paterson, New Jersey. In Paterson, they had stores up and down the streets that sold anything anyone ever wanted. All you had to do was walk outside. In one minute, you could be at a store and have all the candy and toys and baseball cards you could afford to buy. So they did not need a Wall-a-kee Man in New Jersey.

"I bet he doesn't come," Rabbit teased.

"Leave the girls alone, Rabbit," Momma said as she stood outsdside the screen door. "You all need to come in here and eat. Watching won't make him come any faster."

As soon as Momma said those words, the Wall-a-kee Man turned his big white station wagon onto the long, dusty path.

"He's here, Momma!" Sallie Gal shouted. And the three children ran out to his car.

Momma stayed by the door and waited for the Wall-a-kee Man so she could say hello.

The Wall-a-kee Man rolled his window down.

"Afternoon, sir," Sallie Gal and Wild Cat said together.

"My name is Sallie Gal. And this here's Wild Cat."

"Afternoon to you," said the Wall-a-kee Man. "I see you have a friend with you today."

"This is Rabbit," said Sallie Gal. "He's Wild Cat's cousin from up North." Sallie Gal poked Rabbit with her elbow, to remind him of his manners.

"Afternoon, sir," Rabbit said as he stared at the traveling salesman. "He just looks like a regular person,"

Rabbit whispered to Sallie Gal, disappointed. Wild Cat gave him a hard look and held one finger up to her lips.

"Afternoon, sir," Momma called out the front door. She needed to finish folding clothes, so she didn't come all the way out to the car.

"Afternoon, Miss Ida Mae," the Wall-a-kee Man called back. "Anything I can get you today?"

"Not today, but I have fifty cents for you," Momma said. "I will probably need a few things next week."

"That will be fine, Miss Ida Mae," said the Wall-a-kee Man.

Sallie Gal ran to the door and got Momma's fifty cents. And just as she started to close the screen door, Sallie Gal asked Momma if she could ask him about the hair ribbons. Momma said it was okay.

"Pardon me, Mr. Wall-a-kee Man, sir," Sallie Gal said when she got back to the car. "Do you have any hair ribbons for sale in the back of that station wagon?" Sallie Gal forgot his real name, but he didn't seem to mind being called "Mr. Wall-a-kee Man."

Rabbit and Wild Cat stared as he got out of his

car and went into the back. He dug through some things. Then he pulled out a box and opened it. "I do have this big box with uncut ribbons that I sell to beauty salons," he said. "But I can cut you some for two dollars."

Sallie Gal looked at the box of beautiful ribbons. Some were shiny satin. Others were soft velvet. There were polka-dot, plaid, and plain ones. Sallie Gal's eyes filled with tears. She didn't have two dollars for ribbons.

"I think I will have to wait until I have enough," she told the Wall-a-kee Man sadly.

"I'm sorry, Sallie Gal," he said. "Maybe I can just give you a few for now?" He winked.

Momma was still standing at the door. She got

a stern look on her face. "Thank you kindly," she said. "But we don't take charity from *anyone*."

Sallie Gal shook her head. She looked at Momma, and then at the Wall-a-kee Man. "I will just have to wait until I make enough money myself."

The children waved good-bye as the Wall-a-kee Man drove off.

Momma had lunch waiting on the table. The girls barely said a word while they ate their smothered chicken. But Rabbit never stopped talking about the Wall-a-kee Man and all those goods in the back of his car.

After lunch the children were ready to set up the lemonade stand. The menfolks would be coming home from Rocky Mount by three o'clock.

Rabbit carried the wood crate. Wild Cat brought the pickle jars in an old cardboard box. Sallie Gal followed behind them with Momma's pitcher filled with lemonade.

"Careful!" Momma warned. But Sallie Gal was daydreaming, so she didn't hear Momma. Instead, she thought about how good it would feel to have beautiful ribbons in her hair. While she imagined this, she jumped off the porch! But that was a big mistake. The pitcher went flying out of her hands.

Crash!

Rabbit and Wild Cat turned around when they heard the noise. Rabbit held his hands over his eyes. "Sallie Gal!" Wild Cat yelled.

But it was too late. The pitcher was in a million pieces on the ground. Sallie Gal began to cry.

Wild Cat ran to help Sallie Gal.

Sallie Gal looked at her momma's shattered pitcher.

Momma came out to the front porch. She was not happy when she saw her favorite pitcher on the ground, broken into tiny pieces.

"How many times do I have to tell you not to jump over them steps? Now you have broken the pitcher. And you've wasted all

the lemonade and your money. That pitcher cost two dollars at Sears. The lemonade is fifty cents. You owe me two fifty, young lady." Sallie Gal began to cry harder. That was more than her hair ribbons cost! All her hard work was lying in a million pieces on the ground. Momma went over to Sallie Gal. She brushed the dirt off of Sallie Gal's clothes. "Go in the house now and get the last of the lemonade that is in the milk jug. You are in business and you have to keep your word."

No matter what happened, Momma always said "you have to keep your word."

Sallie Gal could see that Momma was upset. But she was trying not to let Sallie Gal know how upset she really was in front of company.

"Stop crying now," Momma said. "I am on my way to wash for Miss Dottie. You go and get the lemonade, and Wild Cat and Rabbit will help you clean up that mess."

Wiping her tears away, Sallie Gal rushed into the house to get the lemonade that was left in the milk jug. Wild Cat and Rabbit helped her sweep up the glass from the ground while Momma watched. Then off Momma went to do her Saturday ironing for Miss Dottie.

Miss Dottie was an old white lady. She lived in the big, pretty white house on the other side of Cumbo Road. It had white fences and pretty white wooden chairs on the porch. Sallie Gal thought it was the prettiest house in the world.

The children set up the lemonade stand and waited for their customers. When the menfolks came by, they bought three more cups of lemonade.

But Sallie Gal was worried. They had made some money. But not nearly enough to pay for the ribbons. And now, she owed Momma. Sallie Gal was beginning to think that her dreams of owning her own ribbons would never come true.

7...The Good Faith Coin

I think we should try something else," Wild Cat said as they walked home from their lemonade stand that day. "Folks do not have five cents for lemonade around here."

"Momma won't let me quit," said Sallie Gal. "Our customers expect us to be here. Now we have to keep our word."

They all walked back home and sat on the porch to wait for Momma. Soon Momma came back from Miss Dottie's house. She was carrying a clothes basket in her arms.

"Why are you back so early, Momma?" Sallie Gal asked.

"Miss Dottie's washing machine broke," Momma replied. "I am going to wash her clothes here."

Momma went to the

side of the house with the basket. She filled the tub with water from the pump. She didn't mention her favorite pitcher.

As Sallie Gal listened to Momma singing, she had an idea.

"I know how we can make some extra money," Sallie Gal said. "We can ask Miss Dottie if we can do some work for her, too. Momma said Miss Dottie is rich. She is eighty-one years old. She can't walk very well. And she can't do much for herself anymore. Let's go knock on Miss Dottie's door. Maybe she will let us help her around her house like Momma does."

"Not me," Rabbit said. "I'm going next door to see what Aunt Annie is making for dessert."

The girls ran down the path and crossed over Cumbo Road into Miss Dottie's yard.

Sallie Gal picked up Miss Dottie's Saturday paper. The paperman had just thrown it into her front yard.

They tiptoed up the steps to Miss Dottie's front door. Sallie Gal knocked like there was a ghost on the other side.

It took Miss Dottie a long time to get to the door. When she finally did open it, she could not see the girls very well. She barely recognized them.

"Good afternoon, Miss Dottie," the girls said together as they looked at her pale skin and her long silver hair that was pinned up in a bun.

"Good afternoon to you both," Miss Dottie answered. "How can I help you today?"

Wild Cat was scared to open her mouth. But not Sallie Gal.

"We are trying to make some extra money. Do you have a job for us?" Sallie Gal asked bravely.

Miss Dottie peeked over her glasses at the girls just like the Wall-a-kee Man always did.

"I heard you were selling lemonade," said Miss Dottie. "I thought that was real good. I wish I felt better. I would have walked down there to get myself a glass or two."

"We have been selling lemonade," Sallie Gal said. "But it's not going so well. We need more work. Could we do some chores for you?"

"Your momma is a good woman," Miss Dottie said. "She does a lot for me. But I got some more things that I need done around here. I like to help folks who are trying to help themselves."

Sallie Gal handed her the newspaper.

"Thank you, girls," Miss Dottie said as she took it gratefully. "You know, I really need my paper brought into the house for me. The paperman always manages to bring it after your momma leaves. I do not always feel well enough to walk out there every day."

Miss Dottie stopped talking for a minute like she was thinking real hard.

"I tell you what, girls. I will give you twenty-five cents a week to bring the paper and to empty my trash can. And just to get you started I will give you a good faith coin."

Miss Dottie walked a few steps away and got

some money out of a porcelain bowl on a small wood table. The girls stared at the pretty table through the screen door. The scent of lavender came outside into their noses. They could see pictures all over the walls and on her pretty tables in every corner. She gave the girls a quarter to share. They could not believe it. That was more than what they made each day at the lemonade stand!

"All right, girls, every evening when you get home, you need to get my paper and leave it where you are standing. I will leave the trash can right there. Just empty it into the old barrel beside the pecan tree in the backyard. Put it with my paper every day. After you do that, sweep the front and back porch for me. I will give you something extra for sweeping."

"Yes, ma'am," the girls agreed.

"Now you all run along and I will look for my paper and clean trash can every day."

"Thank you, Miss Dottie," they said together and they jumped off the long white front porch — just like they did at home.

"Oh! Don't fall, children," Miss Dottie gasped as they flew through the air to the ground.

"See?" Sallie Gal said. "All you have to do is ask." Sallie Gal opened her hand so that she and Wild Cat could see their quarter again.

They ran all the way home to show their mommas their good faith coin.

8 . . . Dollars and Cents

For the rest of the summer, the girls worked hard. Every day when they were finished in the fields, they rushed over to Miss Dottie's house to help with the newspaper and the trash. Then it was time to go back to the lemonade stand to catch the menfolks coming home from the fields. School would be starting soon. Sallie Gal was hoping to have her hair ribbons in time for the first day of school. On Tuesday evening, they found Miss Dottie sitting on her front porch in her rocking chair. She was waiting for Sallie Gal and Wild Cat.

"Evening, Miss Dottie," the girls called out as they raced up the front porch.

"Good evening, girls," she answered. She was knitting a blanket with fine blue yarn. "I was waiting for you two so that I could tell you about my travels."

"What travels?" asked Sallie Gal.

"Travels? Are you going away, Miss Dottie?" asked Wild Cat.

Miss Dottie told them about her plans.

"Every year I go to Newport News to see my brother, Walter. I will be leaving on Friday."

That is bad news, Sallie Gal thought to herself. Miss Dottie couldn't leave. Sallie Gal needed her job to buy her ribbons and the new pitcher, and to pay Momma for the sugar.

Miss Dottie noticed the disappointed look on the girls' faces. "But while I am away," Miss Dottie continued, "I will still want you to pick up my paper. You can put it in this box here." She pointed to the wood box that she used to hold wood in the wintertime. "There won't be trash to take out. But I would still like you to sweep and keep things neat around here. The pinecones need to be raked up and my mail will need to be brought in."

Miss Dottie had another surprise for them. She

took out a box from under her rocking chair. "This is a little gift for you girls to share," she told them. "Now run along before it's too dark to sell your lemonade."

Wild Cat poked Sallie Gal with her elbow. The girls looked at each other with delight.

As Miss Dottie wished them a good evening, she disappeared into her pretty white house and closed the door.

"Open the box," Sallie Gal said as she passed

it over to Wild Cat. She could barely hold it in her hands because she was so excited.

The pink box had white lace on the top and was pretty just like everything else in Miss Dottie's house.

Wild Cat untied the string, and Sallie Gal opened the box. Inside were two small silk bags.

One was filled with quarters, the other with small Chick-O-Sticks candy. Then a note fell out of the box.

"Read it," Sallie Gal said.

Wild Cat slowly opened the note. "What if she's going to fire us when she gets back to Cumbo Road? *You* read it," she said.

Sallie Gal smoothed out the note. Across the

top was engraved with a big "D." Sallie Gal took a breath and read:

Dear Girls,

I am so happy that you are helping me this summer. It is not just the work that I appreciate, but knowing someone is coming by to check on me every day. Give this bag of money to your Momma. I am leaving her with two dollars to pay you while I am away. I will see you on my return.

Miss Dottie

"Two dollars!" Sallie Gal shouted as she grabbed the box out of Wild Cat's hand so that she could get a better look.

"But what will your momma say about her giving us money?" asked Wild Cat.

Sallie Gal hadn't thought about that. What if Momma made her give it back?

The girls ran back across the road to sell their lemonade.

When they were done, they walked home to Sallie Gal's house. They had big smiles on their faces.

Momma was in the kitchen. She was putting the blue plates on the table.

"It's getting dark, Wild Cat," Momma said. "You need to get home. All this extra work in the evening is making you both eat supper too late."

Momma stopped and looked at the girls because they were still whispering to each other, even though Momma had told Wild Cat to go home. Wild Cat never wanted to go home.

"What in the world are you two smiling about?"

The girls looked at each other. Then Sallie Gal and Wild Cat opened the box and showed Momma the candy and the money.

"Miss Dottie is leaving for Newport News tomorrow and she gave us two dollars to give to you so that you would pay us for our work while she is gone away," Wild Cat said.

"Yes, Momma, she did," Sallie Gal added. "We

wanted to know if it is honest to take money before you work."

"Miss Dottie told me all about her trip and the money," Momma said. "That made me very proud. You both have earned her trust."

Sallie Gal and Wild Cat smiled. They were happy that Miss Dottie trusted them.

"Sallie Gal, get the paper and pencil. And get the money jar from the kitchen. Let's figure out how much money you all have. Let's see if there is enough to get your ribbons."

Sallie Gal went into the living room and got the paper and pencil out of the old chest. Then she brought Momma the money jar.

"Annie," she heard Momma yell out of the back window. Aunt Annie was in her kitchen cooking supper, too. "Is it all right for Wild Cat to eat over here tonight?"

"Fine with me," Aunt Annie shouted back. "Willie and Rabbit and I will go on and eat without her."

Momma, Sallie Gal, and Wild Cat all sat down at the table while Momma helped Sallie Gal tally up all their money.

Sallie Gal emptied the money jar. She counted up all the money she and Wild Cat had made from selling the lemonade and from Miss Dottie. The total was $6.50. Sallie Gal and Wild Cat thought that was a lot of money.

"Now, Sallie Gal," Momma said, "divide that by two and give Wild Cat her share." Sallie Gal wasn't allowed to count her field money that Momma kept hidden in her drawer. That was for school clothes.

Sallie Gal handed Wild Cat $3.25. And she kept $3.25 for herself. Then she deducted the $2.00 that she owed Momma for her glass pitcher. And the girls each gave Momma twenty-five cents for their half of the sugar that was used in the lemonade. Then Sallie Gal counted up what was left. There was only one dollar.

Sallie Gal could not believe it. After all of her hard work, she only had one dollar. She barely said a word at supper. Her eyes filled with tears.

"Can I give my money to Sallie Gal for her ribbons?" Wild Cat asked.

"That is real nice of you, Wild Cat," Momma said as she got up to clean the table. "But Sallie Gal needs to take care of this on her own." Momma smiled at Wild Cat and rubbed her hair.

When the dishes were done, Sallie Gal walked Wild Cat outside onto the front porch. The crickets sang loudly. She watched Wild Cat disappear into her house.

When Sallie Gal got back inside, Momma was waiting for her at the kitchen table.

"Sit down, Sallie Gal. I want to talk to you."

Sallie Gal sat down across the table from her momma with her head down.

"Put your head up, my sweet child, and tell me why you think you need to earn your own money for yourself."

"I don't know, Momma."

"It is very simple, child. I want you to work hard for the things that you have, so that you will be able to take care of yourself one day."

"Yes, ma'am," Sallie Gal said.

"Secondly," Momma said, "you have to learn to take care of other people's things. I told you not to jump off that porch. But you didn't listen."

"Yes, ma'am," Sallie Gal said.

Momma put the last piece of lemon pie on a plate with two forks and they shared it.

"You're a good girl, Sallie Gal," Momma said. "We may not have much money. But we are honest folks."

Sallie Gal knew that Momma meant well. But it didn't make her feel any better. And it wasn't helping her to save enough money for her ribbons before school started next week.

Later, as Sallie Gal was climbing into bed, Momma came into Sallie Gal's room.

"Good night, Sallie Gal," Momma said, kissing her softly on her forehead.

"Night, Momma," Sallie Gal said. Then she closed her eyes tight and fell fast asleep.

9 • • • The Secret

The week went by fast. After work on Saturday afternoon, it was once again time for the Wall-a-kee Man to come. Both Sallie Gal and Momma were quiet at breakfast. Sallie Gal still had not saved enough money for her ribbons. But she was excited about getting her school clothes today.

Every week when the Wall-a-kee Man came, he asked Sallie Gal if she had enough money for her ribbons. He knew she was hoping that she would be able to buy them in time for the first day of school. And he knew how hard she had been working for them.

Momma finally spoke. "Cheer up, Sallie Gal. And quit trying to keep up with those half-rich Northern folks of Wild Cat's."

Sallie Gal stared down at her plate to keep the tears from coming. "You are almost nine years old," Momma said. "You just keep making good grades and someday you will go to college and get a good job. Then you will have everything you want. Wild Cat's folks have city jobs and city money. Her ribbons came from her rich relatives in Paterson, New Jersey. We are country folks."

I do not care about all that, Sallie Gal thought to herself as she got up to wash the dishes. *I just want ribbons like Wild Cat's.*

"Hey, Sallie Gal," Wild Cat called as she peeked through the screen door on the back porch. "Good morning, Aunt Ida Mae. Can Sallie Gal and I walk to the field together today?"

"Go on, children," said Momma. "I will be out there in a minute."

The girls walked down the path together hand in hand.

"Hey, wait for me!" Rabbit yelled as he ran behind them.

"We have to hurry home so we can be back in time for the Wall-a-kee Man," Sallie Gal said. Rabbit grabbed Sallie Gal's other hand.

Work went slow today. Sallie Gal wasn't going to be able to get her ribbons, but she was excited about picking out her new dresses and a new pair of shoes. At noontime, the children ran home and took their baths and put on fresh, clean clothes.

By one o'clock, the three of them were waiting on Sallie Gal's front porch.

And then, just like clockwork, the Wall-a-kee Man arrived on Cumbo Road.

"The Wall-a-kee Man is here!" Rabbit called out to Momma, who was on the back porch shelling cornfield beans for supper.

The children crowded around the Wall-a-kee Man's back window when Momma came to the front yard.

Wild Cat looked on. But she never bought anything from the Wall-a-kee Man. Her aunt sent her all the dresses and ribbons she could ever want from Paterson, New Jersey.

"Afternoon, sir," Momma said.

"Afternoon to you, too, Miss Ida Mae. I brought those school dresses for you to look at. And I brought that box of ribbons, too, just in case." The Wall-a-kee Man winked at Sallie Gal.

"Oh, that's nice of you," Momma said. "But we can't afford no ribbons today. Sallie Gal is still saving. Maybe she will get them before Christmas."

"Before Christmas?" Sallie Gal said aloud. Christmas was four months away.

"I'm sorry, Sallie Gal," the Wall-a-kee Man said. "You still have not saved enough money for your ribbons. That's a shame." He knew how badly she had wanted them.

"No, sir, not yet," Sallie Gal said as she looked at the box of ribbons. "But I'm trying real hard to earn the money."

"Now, Sallie Gal, you go ahead and pick two dresses and one pair of shoes," Momma said.

The Wall-a-kee Man got out of the car and laid five dresses on the hood for Sallie Gal to look at. They were all different colors and patterns. Sallie

Gal stroked the dresses like they were gold. Momma held them up high to look at the fabric. Sallie Gal could not resist looking at all the pretty colors in those dresses. Colors that would match her ribbons that she might have by Christmas.

Momma walked around the house to get some money out of the moneybag that was attached to her petticoat with a pin. She would never pull her dress up in front of a man. Not even Uncle Willie.

While Momma was gone, the Wall-a-kee Man opened his box of ribbons. He grabbed his scissors and cut five ribbons. He gave them to Sallie Gal as Rabbit and Wild Cat watched. Sallie Gal couldn't believe it. She finally had ribbons of her own. *But what would Momma say?* No one *ever* disobeyed Momma.

The Wall-a-kee Man winked at Sallie Gal again. "This is between you and me," he said.

He took the ribbons out of Sallie Gal's hand to fold them up and put them in her shoe box. Then he folded the dresses and handed them to her.

The children looked at one another. Then they looked at the Wall-a-kee Man. Momma would not be happy about this. She would *never* let Sallie Gal take anything free from *anybody*.

While Momma paid the Wall-a-kee Man, Sallie Gal ran in the house so that she could hang her new dresses up and put her shoe box away.

Wild Cat and Rabbit followed her inside.

She hung the dresses up neatly in the closet. She put the shoe box with her new shoes and

ribbons under the bed. Then she went into the kitchen for lunch. Rabbit and Wild Cat went home because Uncle Willie had brought them MoonPies for dessert. They promised to bring one for Sallie Gal later. Sallie Gal loved MoonPies. But she wasn't hungry now. She was too busy thinking about Momma. What would Momma say if she knew about those ribbons?

10 . . . Good-bye, Rabbit

Sunday was a sad day for the children. They were sad because after church, Rabbit was going back to Paterson, New Jersey. The girls were going to ride with Rabbit and Mr. Sammy and Uncle Willie to the train station in Rocky Mount. It would be another year before they saw Rabbit again. So the girls knew they wanted to spend their last few minutes together.

At church, Sallie Gal sang in the choir. She wore her good white church dress that Momma got for her. Momma had done extra ironing in order to buy it. Momma mailed Wild Cat's aunt $1.00 a month for ten months to pay for Sallie Gal's church dress.

As Sallie Gal sang, she watched Momma sitting with Aunt Annie in the pews. The menfolks sat in the deacons' pew with the other  deacons. Sallie Gal thought about how hard Momma worked to buy her that dress. And she started to think about the ribbons she had hidden in the shoe box under the bed.

"I'm going to tell Momma about the ribbons as soon as I get home from church," she whispered to Wild Cat when she was supposed to be singing.

"Hush, Sallie Gal," Wild Cat whispered back. "Do you want to get us all in trouble?" Wild Cat sang louder.

After they sang "Jesus Loves Me," Miss Marva called all the little children down front to talk to them during Children's Time. Miss Marva talked to them about being good on the first day of school tomorrow. And she talked to them about the importance of being honest. Sallie Gal hung her head in shame as she listened. Keeping a secret from Momma was not honest.

The moment the service ended, Uncle Willie and Mr. Sammy told the children to hop into the car to take Rabbit to catch the train.

The children laughed and talked all the way to the station. Rabbit had collected cotton bows to take back to Paterson to show to his city cousins. They laughed as cotton bows rolled all over the backseat. They laughed some more as they ate some of the MoonPies that Mr. Sammy gave Rabbit for his trip. Rabbit told the girls that he could teach them to play baseball next summer.

When they got to the train station, everyone got out of the car. There were so many people

waiting for the train. They were all dressed up to go North. It seemed to Sallie Gal that not one little girl was leaving Rocky Mount without a pretty dress and a head full of ribbons.

Finally, it was time for Rabbit to get on the train.

"'Bye, Rabbit," they yelled as the train pulled out from the station. "We'll miss you!"

Tears rolled down Wild Cat's and Sallie Gal's faces. They realized how much they would miss Rabbit and how hard it was to see Rabbit leave. Rabbit waved from the train window. He jumped up and down and made funny faces to make the girls laugh.

But as hard as it was to see Rabbit leave, Sallie Gal knew it was going to be harder to tell Momma about her secret ribbons.

11 . . . The First Day of School

It was barely light outside when Sallie Gal heard the rooster crowing. She knew that meant it was time to get up. The air was chilly, and she had that jumping bean feeling in her stomach that she always got on the first day of school.

She put on her pretty new blue-and-pink dress and her new patent leather shoes. She looked in the mirror. How wonderful her new school outfit would look with a couple of those ribbons in her hair.

But she still had not told Momma about the Wall-a-kee Man's secret present. Maybe if she asked Momma nicely at breakfast, Momma would let her keep them.

"Mornin', Momma," Sallie Gal said as she walked into the kitchen. Her heart was pounding as she got ready to ask.

"Good morning to you, Sallie Gal. You look real pretty in your new clothes."

Sallie Gal smiled and sat down at the table. Momma had made fresh hot biscuits with home-made blueberry jam.

Sallie Gal thought this would be a good time to ask about the ribbons. But just as she opened her mouth to speak, Momma interrupted her.

"And see, Sallie Gal," Momma said. "You look so nice. You did not need ribbons after all."

Sallie Gal lost her nerve. She ate her breakfast. But as she ate, she had a new idea.

Maybe she could just "borrow" those ribbons for the first day of school. She could put them in her book bag. Then she'd tell Momma about them when she got home tonight.

"You do not have to wash dishes today, pretty girl," Momma broke into her thoughts. "It's the first day of school and you need to stay neat."

Sallie Gal took a bite of her breakfast. The warm buttery biscuit melted in her mouth. Sallie Gal felt ashamed. Momma was being so good to her, and Sallie Gal was disobeying her wishes. *Would it be so bad if I just waited one more day before I tell Momma about the Wall-a-kee Man's present to me?* Sallie Gal thought to herself.

Sallie Gal finished her breakfast. As she left the kitchen, she looked at Momma. Momma was singing while she washed the dishes.

Back in her room, Sallie Gal pulled the shoe box out from under her bed. She took those five pretty ribbons and put them into her book bag.

Outside, Wild Cat was already waiting at the end of the path. Her hair was all pressed and ten hair ribbons danced on every one of her long ponytails. There were new ribbons that Sallie Gal had never seen before. Wild Cat looked like she had every ribbon she ever owned on her head.

The school bus was just stopping in front of the house, and the girls got on together. It was good to have a best friend to sit with on the first day of school.

"Hey, Wild Cat," Sallie Gal said as they got on the bus.

"Hey yourself, Sallie Gal," Wild Cat said as they found a seat. "Your dress is pretty. But where are your ribbons?"

"They are here in my bag," Sallie Gal said.

"Sallie Gal!" Wild Cat said. "You haven't told your momma about them ribbons!"

"I'm going to tell her," Sallie Gal whispered. "Now be quiet before someone hears you and tells their momma, who will tell your momma, who will tell my momma."

Wild Cat cupped her hands around Sallie Gal's ear. "You should tell her tonight," Wild Cat whispered. "Because if you don't, you are going to be in big trouble."

When the bus stopped at school, Sallie Gal and Wild Cat rushed off and ran inside to the girls' room.

Sallie Gal opened her book bag. Inside were her five pretty ribbons. One by one, they tied them onto the ends of Sallie Gal's braids. When they were done, Wild Cat stepped back and

looked at Sallie Gal. "You look real pretty," Wild Cat said as she admired Sallie Gal.

Sallie Gal looked in the mirror. She touched each ribbon like it was gold. She shook her head back and forth to make the ribbons bounce like Wild Cat's did. Wearing those ribbons felt so good.

Wild Cat left the girls' room, but Sallie Gal stayed behind. She looked at herself from this side and that side. She smiled. She made funny faces. She looked good. But she felt bad. Wearing those ribbons just didn't feel right. Sallie Gal couldn't keep wearing them. One by one she slowly pulled them off her braids. Neatly, she put them back into her old canvas book bag. She'd have to tell Momma about them tonight.

12 • • • The Lesson

That night, Momma and Sallie Gal sat down together at the supper table.

"How was your first day of school, child?" Momma asked.

"Fine," Sallie Gal said.

Sallie Gal took a deep breath. She looked at her plate. She looked at Momma. She was all ready to tell Momma about the ribbons. But Momma interrupted her.

"I'll bet you got a lot of compliments on your pretty dress and shoes," Momma said.

Sallie Gal closed her mouth and nodded. Then she stared down at her plate. *I have to tell her now,* Sallie Gal thought to herself. She opened her mouth to speak, but no words came out. Instead, she ate her corn bread. She felt like she was eating a plate full of shame.

All week, Sallie Gal brought her hair ribbons to school in her old canvas book bag. But she just couldn't wear them. And every night, she tried to tell Momma. But she couldn't.

On Friday night, Wild Cat came over for dinner. As they ate, Wild Cat kicked Sallie Gal under the table and made faces.

"Tell her!" Wild Cat moved her lips every time Momma looked the other way.

By the end of dinner, Sallie Gal still had not told Momma. She thought and thought. She still had one dollar left from her extra jobs. Perhaps she could use that to pay for the five ribbons.

"What if I just pay the Wall-a-kee Man the

money I owe him for the ribbons?" Sallie Gal whispered to Wild Cat as they washed the dishes.

"You'll still have to tell your momma," said Wild Cat.

"Yes," said Sallie Gal. "I will still need to tell her."

On Saturday, there was no field work to be done. Not 'til the cotton was ready for picking. So Sallie Gal and Wild Cat played One, Two, Three — Red Light! in the front yard. Sallie Gal was better at double Dutch than Wild Cat. But Wild Cat was better at Red Light.

With butterflies in her stomach, Sallie Gal waited for the Wall-a-kee Man as she played with Wild Cat. She had the money in her pocket to pay him for the ribbons he had given her.

Wild Cat went first, as Sallie Gal held her hands

tight over her eyes. Then Wild Cat walked away, trying hard to make sure Sallie Gal did not catch her moving. Together, they yelled, "*One, two, three — red light!*"

Quickly Sallie Gal turned around. "Got you!" she said.

"No, you did not," Wild Cat said. "I am as still as a mouse."

At one o'clock sharp, the Wall-a-kee Man's station wagon pulled up in front of the house. Sallie Gal ran to his car. She left Wild Cat standing frozen in her red light position.

Sallie Gal put her hands in her pocket. She felt the money, but before she could say one word to the Wall-a-kee Man, Momma came outside.

"Afternoon, sir," Momma said while she was making her way to his car.

"Evening, ladies," he said as he rolled his window down to get a good look at his best customer on Cumbo Road.

Momma was glad to see him. "I need to get some sugar to make a birthday cake for Sallie Gal. Her ninth birthday is tomorrow."

Now Sallie Gal felt terrible. With Momma

there she couldn't pay the Wall-a-kee Man for her ribbons. She could not tell Momma that she had them. And now Momma was buying extra sugar for her birthday. Extra sugar that they could not afford. Sallie Gal knew that her momma never got extra stuff "on time." Momma said that her daddy's daddy said that the best way to live a long life is to stay out of debt. Debt, he said, will make you worry yourself to an early grave.

Momma looked into the back of the Wall-a-kee Man's car window. She saw all the pretty ribbons that he had taken out of the box and hung in the back window.

"You know what, sir," said Momma. "I think it's time for Sallie Gal to get those hair ribbons she wants so bad."

Sallie Gal did not move. What could she do? She had to tell Momma now.

"Momma, please do not buy the ribbons," Sallie Gal said.

Momma looked surprised. "But, Sallie Gal, I thought you really wanted hair ribbons to match your new school dresses. Why did you change your mind?"

Sallie Gal looked down at the grass. "I do want the ribbons, Momma. But I already have some," she said.

The Wall-a-kee Man looked at Sallie Gal. Sallie Gal began to cry. Suddenly he understood. She had not told her momma about their secret.

"You have ribbons?" Momma asked, surprised. "You mean you borrowed some from Wild Cat even after I told you that you could not?"

"No, Momma, I did not borrow them from Wild Cat. Last week the Wall-a-kee Man gave them to me."

"Gave them to you?" asked Momma. "You know we don't take charity, Sallie Gal."

Poor Mr. Wall-a-kee Man. He looked so sad. Suddenly he knew that he was wrong as two left shoes to give Sallie Gal those ribbons.

Momma turned to the Wall-a-kee Man. "Sir, I know you mean well, but we do not take charity from *anyone*."

"I'm real sorry, Miss Ida Mae. I gave Sallie Gal the ribbons because I wanted to make her happy and to save you some money. This will never happen again."

Momma wasn't pleased. Even after he apologized. But she always said you have to give a person a second chance to make a wrong right.

"That is all you can do, Mr. Wall-a-kee Man. And you make *sure* this never happens again." Momma's pride always outweighed her anger.

Wild Cat didn't say one word. She never did when Sallie Gal was in trouble.

Sallie Gal looked at Momma.

"I'm real sorry, Momma. I was just going to pay him. I have one dollar right here in my pocket."

Sallie Gal reached in her pocket and pulled out her money. Momma did not look at the money.

She did not look at Sallie Gal. She nodded her head toward the house and Sallie Gal knew what she had to do. She hung her head and walked into the house. Wild Cat followed her.

When Sallie Gal returned, she gave all of her beautiful secret ribbons back to the Wall-a-kee Man.

As they watched the Wall-a-kee Man drive down the road, Sallie Gal felt sad. She also felt relieved. She no longer had a secret from Momma. But now she would *never* have her ribbons.

13 . . . Happy Birthday

Sunday morning, Momma walked past Sallie Gal in the hallway. Momma was in a big hurry. Her arms were full with Sallie Gal's clothes.

"Good morning, Birthday Girl."

"Good morning, Momma."

Sallie Gal was worried. Today was her birthday. But she wasn't sure if her punishment was over. Momma told her that she would have to work for Miss Dottie for free next Saturday. And yesterday she wasn't allowed to play with Wild Cat for the rest of the day. Worst of all, Momma had not said *anything* else about a birthday party.

Silently, Sallie Gal followed Momma into the bedroom. Momma laid out Sallie Gal's Sunday clothes on the bed, and she polished Sallie Gal's shoes with a biscuit from last night's supper.

"Are we going to church?" Sallie Gal asked.

"No, not today, Sallie Gal," answered Momma. "Today is your birthday and we are having a little party."

"Even though I did wrong?"

"Yes, even though you did wrong. You been punished enough."

Sallie Gal hugged Momma. Then she jumped on the bed beside her clothes. *When I grow up*, Sallie Gal thought, *I will get Momma that polka-dot bedspread from the Wall-a-kee Man.*

Momma looked at Sallie Gal. "Come on now, child, let's eat breakfast."

Sallie Gal followed Momma into the kitchen. Momma had set the table for her birthday with hot biscuits and molasses. They ate a nice breakfast together. Then they got ready for the party. As they worked, Momma sang church songs. Sallie Gal joined her when she knew the words. It was turning out to be a good day after all.

After lunch, it was time for the party to start.

Uncle Willie, Aunt Annie, and Wild Cat all came to join the celebration.

There was a pile of birthday gifts in the middle of the table. Sallie Gal couldn't wait to open them. Momma gave Sallie Gal the first box. It was wrapped in yellow paper. Sallie Gal tore it off. It was from Uncle Willie and Aunt Annie.

"A new book bag!" Sallie Gal shouted. She wrapped her arms around Uncle Willie's long legs and Aunt Annie's apron. "Thank you!" she said with a great big smile.

Then she picked up a smaller package. It was wrapped in the funny papers from Miss Dottie's *Northampton County News.* "It's from me," Wild Cat told her. She tore the newspaper off her gift. "A *real* jump rope!" Sallie Gal cried. The best friends hugged. There were two more boxes left to open. They both were wrapped in brown paper. "This one came all the way from Paterson, New Jersey," said Aunt Annie.

"Rabbit!" Sallie Gal and Wild Cat shouted together. Sallie Gal opened it as fast as she could. It was a baseball.

"Now we will have a baseball to play with when Rabbit comes next year," Sallie Gal said.

"And Rabbit can play baseball with us when he comes next year!" said Wild Cat.

As Sallie Gal opened the next package, she noticed that it did not have a return address on it.

"Who is it from?" Uncle Willie asked as an envelope fell out of the box.

Sallie Gal tore it open. There was a note inside. "It's from Papa," she said quietly. Then she read her birthday message.

Dear Sallie Gal,

I am so sorry that I missed your birthday party.

I really wanted to come, but I could not get a leave of absence. You are my favorite girl in the world. Your momma told me about your hard work this summer and I wanted to send a little something to help you get a few extra things for yourself. I hope you have a fun birthday.

Love, Papa

Tears came to Sallie Gal's eyes. She missed her papa, and she wished he was there. Then the three dollar bills fell out of the envelope. The girls jumped up and down for joy.

Sallie Gal could not believe what a good birthday she was having. Now she had more than enough money to buy her ribbons!

Momma put the cake on the table. It was lemon cake with lemon icing. Sallie Gal's favorite. They lit the candles and everyone joined in to sing "Happy Birthday." Uncle Willie hit a high note and everyone laughed.

"Make a wish," Momma said.

Sallie Gal shut her eyes tight. She knew exactly what she was going to wish for. She took a deep breath and blew out every last candle.

Then there was a knock at the front door.

"Who could that be?" Momma said. Their friends always used the side door when visiting. Momma went to answer the door. "You have a guest!" she called out to Sallie Gal.

Sallie Gal ran through the house. *Who had come to visit at the front door?* she wondered. Wild Cat followed. When she got to the door, Sallie Gal could not believe her eyes. It was the Wall-a-kee Man!

"Happy birthday, Sallie Gal," he said. "Miss Ida Mae, I just left our Sunday church service in Tarboro, and I thought I would stop by. I just wanted to say how sorry I am again about yesterday, and to ask you if I can give Sallie Gal a gift the proper way. She works so hard. And she is such a wonderful girl. It's from Miss Dottie and me."

Momma smiled. "That is fine, sir, and I thank you. Would you like to stay a while?" Momma asked the Wall-a-kee Man.

"Well," the Wall-a-kee Man said, "that cake looks mighty good. I think I will."

Momma walked out on the porch and offered him a chair. Aunt Annie and Uncle Willie came to the doorway to see who the visitor was.

"You look so pretty, Sallie Gal," the Wall-a-kee Man said. Then he handed her a beautiful box. It was wrapped in a piece of white lace.

Sallie Gal opened the gift that was from Miss Dottie and the Wall-a-kee Man. Inside was a bottle of lavender perfume. The girls sprayed each other on the neck with the lavender and laughed hard.

Sallie Gal loved all of her gifts. She knew how lucky she was to have such good friends and family. But she still did not have her ribbons. Maybe Momma would let her buy them now. She went inside the house to her bedroom. Then she opened her drawer and took out the dollar she earned. She put it with the $3.00 from Papa.

"Momma," she said when she came back out. "I am sorry about yesterday. If my punishment is over, may I buy my ribbons now?"

Momma smiled at Sallie Gal. Tears came to her eyes. She gave Sallie Gal a big, long hug. "Yes, Sallie Gal," Momma said. "I was saving this surprise for you, but I will tell you now. I bought a beautiful new vase from the Wall-a-kee Man, and it only cost one dollar. Here is your dollar back. Now you can buy the ribbons with all your own money!"

Sallie Gal beamed with pride as she gave the Wall-a-kee Man her own two dollars. She had earned every penny of it herself!

The Wall-a-kee Man gave her a big smile and went out to the car to get her ribbons.

When Sallie Gal opened the box, it was so full of ribbons in every color that some of them fell to the ground.

Sallie Gal could not believe that they were all hers to keep. She and Wild Cat put a ribbon on each one of Sallie Gal's braids!

Sallie Gal ran inside to get her new jump rope. They pulled the Wall-a-kee Man away from the grown-ups he was talking to so that she and Wild Cat could show him how to turn the rope for double Dutch.

Aunt Annie went back inside and brought the ice cream and cake out onto the porch. As Sallie Gal and Wild Cat jumped double Dutch, the grown folks sat all evening and talked and watched the children play.

"Nine, nine, I'm doing fine!" Sallie Gal sang as loud as she could. Sallie Gal's feet crisscrossed as fast as lightning. She jumped like she had rubber legs. She could feel her ribbons flying high up into the air. She shook her head like Wild Cat always did when she was showing off. To the left. To the right. Round and round! Her ribbons bounced and twirled and flew at the ends of her braids.

Sallie Gal's dream had come true. Wild Cat cheered. Everyone clapped their hands with joy. And Sallie Gal had the happiest birthday she'd ever had.

AUTHOR'S NOTE

I was born in an old brown wooden house on Rehobeth Road (in Rich Square, North Carolina) only one fourth of a mile from Cumbo Road, where this story is set.

Most of the African American people who lived there sharecropped for the white people who owned most of the land. Even the children, including myself, chopped in the summertime. The older children picked cotton in the fall, while we tagged along, putting in a few pieces as we tried to keep up with the adults who were walking, talking, and picking fast. During the week, we chopped from 6:00 A.M. to 6:00 P.M. On Saturday, we stopped working at noon. Just in time to see the Wall-a-kee Man driving down the road.

I cannot remember how old I was when I first saw the Wall-a-kee Man. I really cannot remember a time in my young life on Rehobeth Road when he did not come by to sell goods to my mother, my grandmother, and the rest of the African American people who lived in our neighborhood. He went to the few white people who lived in houses on Rehobeth Road and Cumbo, too, but the "coloreds" were his best customers.

It was a way of life for him to come by on Saturdays. Just like breathing. On Saturday morning, rain, sleet, or snow the Wall-a-kee Man showed up. He was a traveling salesman for J. R. Watkins Medical Company, out of Minnesota, which was founded in the 1800s. They had hundreds of salesmen who sold goods to people in rural areas who had little means of transportation. Originally they only sold medical products. But the salesman who came to our area quickly realized that there was a market for everything from sugar to clothing.

No matter what Momma was doing, she stopped her chores when the Wall-a-kee Man came. If she was washing, she stopped the washer, dried her hands, and came to buy something from him. Sometimes, she just came outside to say hello and to pay a little money on the goodies she'd purchased the week before.

Even if she did not need anything and there was no payment to make, she still stopped whatever she was doing and came out to say, "Afternoon, sir."

"Afternoon, Mer," he would respond. Some of the people on Rehobeth Road called my mother Mer, short for Mary Maless.

The children spoke to the Wall-a-kee Man, but we were not allowed to approach his car to shop unless we had permission from Momma. When he drove into the yard, we jumped up and down with excitement. When he left, we waved good-bye and wondered what Momma had in the brown paper bag. Surely she had something sweet for us. Momma would buy bedspreads for the bed and food to put on the table, but if she had any extra money, she would cool our sweet tooth with a piece of candy or two.

Like clockwork, he came. He was a part of our community. Rehobeth and Cumbo roads were filled with rituals in the old days, as they are today. And if there was only one thing we knew for sure, it was this: If it was Saturday, the Wall-a-kee Man was coming.

Note: The expression "cotton bow" is a regional term for "cotton boll."